LEGENDS

ANTHONY HOROWITZ

DEATH, AND THE UNDERWORLD

Illustrated by Thomas Yeates

MACMILLAN CHILDREN'S BOOKS

First published 2011 by Macmillan Children's Books
a division of Macmillan Publishers Limited
20 New Wharf Road, London N1 9RR
Basingstoke and Oxford
Associated companies throughout the world
www.panmacmillan.com

ISBN 978-0-330-51018-9

Text copyright © Anthony Horowitz 1985, 2011
Illustrations copyright © Thomas Yeates 2011

The right of Anthony Horowitz and Thomas Yeates to be identified as
the author and illustrator of this work has been asserted by them in
accordance with the Copyright, Designs and Patents Act 1988.

All rights reserved. No part of this publication may be
reproduced, stored in or introduced into a retrieval system, or
transmitted, in any form or by any means (electronic, mechanical,
photocopying, recording or otherwise), without the prior written
permission of the publisher. Any person who does any unauthorized
act in relation to this publication may be liable to criminal prosecution
and civil claims for damages.

1 3 5 7 9 8 6 4 2

A CIP catalogue record for this book is available from
the British Library.

Printed and bound in the UK by CPI Mackays, Chatham ME5 8TD

This book is sold subject to the condition that it shall not,
by way of trade or otherwise, be lent, resold, hired out,
or otherwise circulated without the publisher's prior consent
in any form of binding or cover other than that in which
it is published and without a similar condition including this
condition being imposed on the subsequent purchaser.

LEGENDS

DEATH, AND THE UNDERWORLD

CONTENTS

INTRODUCTION

Death and the Underworld is probably not the most cheerful title for a book, but my third collection of myths and legends taken from around the world focuses on exactly that. Here we have Hades (Greece), the giant Owuo (West Africa) and Yama (India) – all gods of death, but as different as the cultures from which they came.

Let's talk a bit about death. If you're reading this book you're probably about fourteen or fifteen years old – maybe younger – and the idea that your life will one day come to an end probably hasn't occurred to you and, anyway, it's so far away it doesn't matter. Unfortunately I'm the other side of fifty, so I think about it rather more. What will happen? Will it just be like going to sleep – only a whole lot longer? Or will it be more exciting than that. J. M. Barrie, the author of *Peter Pan*, called death an 'awfully big adventure', and who can say he isn't right?

When I first began this collection thirty years ago, I was determined to go further than ancient Athens for my source material. As always I have tried to tell these stories as if for the first time and have added a few thoughts and descriptions of my own, but I hope I have remained true to the spirit of the originals, which have, after all, lasted hundreds if not thousands of years. And I think it's fascinating to revisit a story like 'Death and the Boy', which may not be quite as logical nor make quite as much sense as the much better-known tale of 'Orpheus in the Underworld' – the hero doesn't even have a name – but which does somehow tell us how the people of Togoland once saw the universe.

I was very glad to include the story of Nornagest – his death seems to me to represent a turning point between the ancient and the modern worlds. There was no place any more for the old gods. They had to be banished to make way for the new belief of Christianity. King Olaf Tryggvason was a real person, by the way, and although not much is known about him, it seems that he was a thoroughly nasty piece of work. He killed one enemy by forcing a snake down their throat and another by piling up a heap of hot coals on their stomach. And all in the name of religion!

So that's *Death and the Underworld*. I hope you enjoy the book and that it's a long time before you encounter either of them.

Anthony Horowitz

DEATH AND THE BOY

West African

Death and the Boy

West Africa was gripped by the unrelenting hand of famine. Its arid breath whispered over the land, blighting the crops and blistering the livestock. Its shadow fell across the villages, stretching ever further in the remorseless sunlight. The water holes shrivelled and dried up. The mud hardened then cracked. Wherever the people went, black flies followed, sucking the last drops

of moisture from the corners of their eyes and mouths. If famine was the king, the flies were its most loyal knights.

It was a cruel time. Every minute of every day became an exhausting struggle to find food, to break into the unyielding earth for water, to save the pathetically withered things that had been root vegetables or plants. The people struggled and prayed for rain. They knew they would survive. They had been through it all before.

But in one village there was a young boy who could work no longer. He had not eaten meat for so long (he thought) that he had forgotten what it tasted like. He was tired of the daily labouring, tired of seeing the blank determination that hung on the faces of his friends and relatives. And so one day he left the village, slipping away into the jungle to find his fortune – or at the very least, to renew his acquaintance with the flavour of meat.

For three days he walked without

stumbling on so much as a parrot that he might pop into a pot. But on the third day, just as he was about to turn round and go home again, he came across something very peculiar. There were forty or fifty black ropes – at least, they looked like ropes – running along the jungle floor. The ropes ran in both directions for as far as he could see. Acting on impulse, puzzled as to what they might be, the boy decided to follow them and accordingly turned to the left.

He walked for more than a mile before the mystery was explained. The ropes weren't ropes at all. They were hair. And the boy had followed them to the scalp of their owner.

It was, of course, a giant. He was sitting outside a mud hut (from a distance, the boy had mistaken the hut for a small mountain) fast asleep. The giant was pitch black, the same colour as his remarkable hair, and this made the whiteness of his teeth seem all the more brilliant. These were the first things the boy noticed. The second was that despite the famine, the giant looked remarkably well fed.

The boy was just wondering whether he should stay where he was or head for home as fast as his feet would carry him when he became aware of a movement. The giant's eyes had opened, and he was regarding the boy with a sort of tired puzzlement.

'What are you?' he demanded, yawning.

'Please, sir . . . I'm a boy,' the boy said. 'I didn't mean to wake you up. I was looking for meat.'

'How did you find me?'

'Well, sir . . . I followed your hair.'

'You mean, you've been haring through the jungle?'

Death and the Boy

The giant roared with laughter at his own joke, the sound making the ground vibrate. The boy laughed too, although he hadn't actually thought it was very funny. But then, when somebody one hundred times as big as you makes a joke, it's probably a good idea to laugh.

'If you want meat,' the giant said, when he had calmed down, 'I will give it to you. But you will have to earn it. You will have to stay here and work for me.'

And so the boy remained, sweeping and chopping wood for the fire. And in return for these simple tasks, the giant was true to his word and fed him with as much steak as he could eat.

There came a time, however, when the boy became homesick. It had been months since he had seen his parents and his village and so he asked the giant for permission to take a short holiday.

'Of course,' the giant said. 'But you must send me someone to take your place while you're gone.'

'I'll do that,' the boy promised and, packing his bag full of meat for the journey, he set off through the jungle.

His family was delighted to see him when he got back and were astonished to find him looking so plump and healthy. His brother in particular pressed him to say what had happened.

'If you really want to know,' the boy told him, 'I can help you. How would you like a job where in return for the lightest of tasks you got more meat than you knew what to do with?'

'I'd love it!' the brother said.

Then the boy told him about the giant and the hut in the jungle. The brother naturally leaped at the opportunity to take his place and set off at once.

'By the way,' he asked, just before

he left, 'what is this giant of yours called?'

'His name is Owuo,' the boy said.

Now Owuo is a West African word. And it means 'death'.

Six weeks passed; more than enough time to cure the boy's homesickness. The trouble with home was that there still wasn't any meat and worse still, his parents expected him to join in the household chores, which meant far harder work than he had got used to with Owuo. So one day he packed his bag

again and followed the path of hair back to the giant's hut.

He had expected to see his brother there, but to his surprise there was no sign of him. The giant, however, was unperturbed.

'He left a couple of days ago,' he explained. 'Like you, he got homesick. I'm surprised you didn't cross paths in the jungle.'

'I'd have thought he'd have waited for me,' the boy said.

'Forget him!' the giant cried. 'I've been waiting to tell you a new joke. Have you heard the one about the Krachian, the Salagan and the Zulu . . .?'

Time passed as pleasantly as it had before. The giant seemed perfectly content even though the boy did precious little work. And meanwhile the boy ate so much meat that he became quite fat. But once again, the only fly in the ointment was that he missed his brother and his parents. So, gathering his courage, he asked the giant if he could be allowed a second holiday.

'Very well!' the giant said. 'But this time I wonder if you could send me a young girl to take your place? In fact –' and here he winked – 'I have it in mind to take her as my wife. If you could rustle up a pretty girl, I'd like to marinate her.'

'Did you say . . . marinate her, sir?' the boy asked.

'Did I?' The giant coughed and blushed. 'I meant marry her. I want to marry her!'

It was with a slight but indistinct feeling of uneasiness that the boy returned to his village. This time he was greeted with a little less pleasure. For his brother had disappeared. Despite what the giant had said, he had never returned home.

Nonetheless, the boy didn't mention the giant – for he was afraid that he would be forbidden to return to the hut if he did. It was only when he was talking to his sister one evening that he mentioned Owuo and in particular his desire for a wife.

'A wife?' the sister repeated. 'If I were the

wife of this Owuo, I would never have to work again. Like you, I could eat meat all day long.'

'Yes, but—' the boy began uncertainly.

'How do I find him?' the sister interrupted.

Although the boy still felt uneasy about it, his sister forced him to describe the path of hair, and the next morning she left, taking a servant with her.

This time the boy only waited a fortnight before he followed her back to the giant's hut. It was with a sinking feeling that he found Owuo sitting by himself, gnawing a bone.

'You're back early,' the giant said.

'Yes,' the boy replied. 'My sister . . .?'

'I haven't seen her or her servant for a week.' The giant tossed the bone over his shoulder. 'But I expect they'll turn up soon. Get yourself some supper, my boy. You must be hungry after your journey.'

The boy wasn't hungry, but nodding his thanks, he went into the giant's hut where

the meat was usually hung, out
of the sun. As always, the ground
was littered with bones and it was as
he stepped over these that he stopped, a
wave of ice rippling through his body. His
eyes bulged. His hair stood on end. The skin
at the back of his neck tried to creep on to
his shoulders.

There was a bracelet made of red beads
around one of the bones. He would have
recognized it anywhere, for he had made it
himself. He had once given it to his sister as
a birthday present.

That night, as soon as it was dark, the

boy tiptoed away from the hut and then, his heart pounding, raced through the jungle, crashing blindly into the undergrowth, hardly caring where he went. He didn't stop until he had somehow reached his village and then he was so breathless that it was an hour before he could tell his parents what had happened.

The grief of the villagers at the loss of three lives was mingled with horror when they heard how Owuo had dealt with his victims. As one, they marched into the jungle, carrying with them flaming torches to light their way. The boy went with them for although nobody had said as much, he

15

knew that he was to blame, and there was nothing he would not do to make amends.

It was by the light of the torches that they came upon the hair, more like snakes now than ropes as it twisted through the night. Then the boy had an idea.

'Owuo is too big for us to fight,' he cried. 'Let the fire do our work for us.'

And so saying, he seized a torch and thrust it into the hair.

Like a burning fuse, the hair hissed and crackled, carrying the fire on

a winding path
through the jungle.
The villagers followed
close behind. And so it was
that they arrived at the hut
just in time to see Owuo erupt in
flames. One moment he was sleeping
peacefully, the next he had disappeared in a
crimson inferno. His screams were like the
wind in a thunderstorm. But then it was all
over and only a great heap of white powder
showed where he had lain.

17

However, rummaging around in the ashes, the boy came upon a small bottle that Owuo had kept hidden in the very hair that had been his undoing. There were just four drops of a transparent liquid in the bottle and realizing that whatever it was must be magic, he allowed three of them to fall on the bones in the giant's hut. In an instant, to the great rejoicing of the villagers, his brother, his sister and the servant-girl sprang to life, apparently none the worse for having been chewed up, swallowed and digested.

'Now – what shall I do with the last drop?' the boy asked.

'Wait . . .' his father said.

'No!' his mother cried.

'You idiot!' the villagers yelled.

For the boy had upturned the bottle over the ashes of the giant.

Everyone stared.

A puddle formed in the middle of the ashes, bubbling and hissing. A wisp of smoke curled poisonously upwards, writhing in the moonlight. Slowly, hideously, an eye took shape. It opened, then gazed balefully at the boy who staggered back, terrified.

But that was all. Although the potion was powerful enough to restore a human life, it could manage no more than one eye of the giant.

In Togoland, where this myth originated, the people believe that the eye is still there, and that whenever it blinks, someone, somewhere in the world, dies. And because there is so much dust in the country, it blinks often. And one day, they say, the eye will blink for you . . .

ORPHEUS IN THE UNDERWORLD

Greek

Orpheus in the Underworld

Amongst the Argonauts who had sailed with Jason in pursuit of the fabled Golden Fleece there had been one hero who carried neither sword nor shield, neither spear nor bow. His name was Orpheus and he was famed throughout Ancient Greece as a poet and musician. When Orpheus sang, people stopped whatever they were doing and smiled in wonderment. Wild animals became tame. Even the trees and the stones

would move from where they stood in order to be nearer to the sound.

Orpheus was the son of a Thracian king. His mother was one of the nine Muses: Calliope, the spirit of poetry and eloquence. His lyre had been given to him by Apollo himself and with the Muses as his teachers he had learned to play music in a way that is beyond description. But if you had ever heard him, it is a sound you would never have forgotten.

After his return from the kingdom of Colchis (where Jason was able to steal the Golden Fleece only after Orpheus had lulled the dragon that guarded it to sleep) he decided to settle down and get married. His young wife was called Eurydice. She was a nymph whom he loved very dearly and for a long time the two of them were as happy as two people can possibly be.

But then came the day when a friend called Aristaeus came to stay and took Eurydice for a walk in the fields. This Aristaeus was a famous huntsman, a bee-keeper and the father of Actaeon. It was a warm, sunny day. Orpheus had stayed in the house to practise a new tune. The two of them were alone.

They had reached a quiet spot where the field dipped down beside a wood when Aristaeus suddenly seized hold of Eurydice, kissed her passionately and told her that he had always loved her, that he wanted to marry her, that he had only come in the hope of persuading her to run away with him. At first Eurydice thought he was joking. Then, when she saw the madness in his eyes, she called out for help. But nobody heard. Finally she managed to break free and with Aristaeus close behind her, she raced back towards the house.

She might well have got there safely, for already Aristaeus regretted what he had done. Even as he ran after her, he shouted for her forgiveness. But Eurydice wouldn't listen. His cries only made her run all the faster, barely looking where she was going. And so

it was that she failed to see an emerald snake twisting through the grass. Her bare foot trod on its tail. It coiled round and sank its fangs into her ankle. In her panic, Eurydice hardly felt the pain but continued to run until she became giddy. A numbing coldness spread through her body. The ground rushed up at her and the light of the sun shimmered and went out. By the time Aristaeus caught up with her, she was dead.

When Orpheus was told what had happened, a terrible pallor came into his face as though part of him had died as well. For three days he stayed in his house, refusing both food and water. On the fourth day he appeared again, dressed in the same clothes he had worn on his adventures with the Argonauts, his lute in his hands. It was dawn when he left the house. Nobody saw him as he walked down the path and crossed the very field where his beloved Eurydice

had fallen. For many months, nobody saw him again.

His journey took him to the very edge of the world, through countries so strange and distant that they had yet to be given names. He climbed mountains and crossed deserts. Neither hunger nor thirst could stop him, neither burning sun nor freezing snow. He came to a great ocean and set sail in a fragile boat, trusting to the wind to blow him even further to the West. He sailed for a long, long time. He sailed until the day and the night merged into an unbroken greyness and time lost its meaning. But at last he arrived on the other side and found himself on the shores of Hades, the home of the dead.

Nothing grew there. The poplar trees that lined the shore were black, their leaves as dry as dust. The soil was barren, the land cloaked in perpetual night. Not a breath of wind touched Orpheus as he walked through the immense silence towards the single mountain that dominated the coast.

He alone was alive and being alive had no place there.

He came to a pair of gates a mile high, the spiked points rising higher than the mountain, brushing the very clouds. The gates were made of black iron, with iron skulls set between the twisting bars. A brazier burned on each side, the flames as cold as ice. Behind the gates he could just make out an enormous cavern, a great circle of darkness. This was the entrance to Hades. And it was guarded.

A dog lumbered out of the shadows, growling softly at Orpheus, with not one but three heads. Its three mouths hung open, black venom dripping over needle-sharp teeth. Its six eyes blinked poisonously. The dog was huge, bigger than a horse. Its black fur hung in knots off its deformed body as if it had rolled in tar.

Now it squatted, preparing to pounce. One of the heads began to howl, the horrible sound rising to a pitch and threatening to

crack open the mountain itself. The other heads snapped at the air, the necks straining, the eyes bulging with hatred and fear.

Slowly, Orpheus lifted the lyre. The howling stopped. One of the heads sniffed at him suspiciously. He began to play.

The sound was tiny, lost in that eternal wilderness, but still the dog heard it. It fell silent and the muscles in its neck relaxed. One of the heads made a last protest, barking feebly, but at once the other two turned on it, tearing at its ears and cheeks with their teeth. It yelped, then listened quietly. Orpheus continued to play, louder now, the music swelling up like

a blossom opening. Never had such a sound been heard at the gateway of Hades. The dog sank to the ground. Something close to pleasure flickered in its yellow eyes. Two of the heads nodded and fell asleep. The third sighed, then joined them. Orpheus played until he reached the end of the song. By then the dog was sound asleep, its tail twitching, its three heads snoring in unison. Gently, he stepped round it. The gates opened and he passed through.

A wide, sandy road led from the mouth of the cave, sloping ever more steeply downhill with every step. The way was lit by silver flames, burning in cornet-shaped braziers attached to the walls. The further Orpheus went, the more heavily he felt the weight of the earth and stone bearing down on him. He thought he must have reached the very centre of the world when he heard the sound of running water, turned a corner and saw a river sparkling eerily as it raced through a vast subterranean cavern.

Orpheus in the Underworld

A figure was standing beside a low, flat boat and as Orpheus drew nearer he saw that it was an old man with spectacles, dressed in a threadbare grey coat and woollen mittens. The boat was shaped like a fish with a head at one end and a tail at the other. The oars had been painted to look like the wings of a dragonfly.

'Who are you?' the old man demanded, taking off his spectacles and wiping them on his sleeve. 'I wasn't told anyone was coming today – not that anyone tells me anything, of course. Wait a minute!' He put the glasses back on and peered at Orpheus with bloodshot eyes. 'You're not even dead!' he exclaimed. 'Really, this is most irregular. You're not dead! At least, you don't look dead.' He reached out with a finger and poked Orpheus. 'Yes! You're alive! Ugh! Really! Well!' And he sat down in a heap.

Orpheus bent over him. 'Who are you?' he asked.

'Charon,' the old man said. 'I run the ferry

to Hades. This is the River Acheron and that
is my ferry. But I only take dead people. It's in
my contract. There must be some mistake,
you know.' He looked up sharply. 'How did
you get past Cerberus?'

'Cerberus?' Orpheus asked.

'The dog. The three-headed dog! I bet he
wasn't pleased to see you.'

'He wasn't.'

'Well of course he wasn't. If you'd have been dead, he'd have been delighted to see you. Happy to let you in, not so happy to let you out – that's Cerberus. Now, what do you want?'

'Will you take me over the Acheron?' Orpheus said.

'Certainly not! You're alive.'

'But I want to cross all the same.'

'Against the rules. More than my job's worth. Sorry. Goodbye!'

Orpheus looked at the river. He would have swum but the water was flowing far too swiftly. He turned back to Charon.

'I'll tell you what,' he said. 'If I can make you smile, then will you take me across?'

'Smile?' Charon sniffed. 'I haven't smiled for seven thousand years – and then it was only due to a misunderstanding. If you can make me smile, I'll take you across for nothing, and that's something I never do. One obol is what it costs. One obol for a one-way ticket. But I'll take you for nothing.'

So once again Orpheus lifted his lyre. This time he chose a song that he knew would appeal to the old miser, a song about King Midas whose touch turned anything to gold. At first Charon merely yawned and scratched under his chin. But as the music continued, the edges of his mouth began to twitch. He shook his head and pretended to pick his teeth, but it was useless. When

Orpheus sang how King Midas almost starved because all his food turned to gold before he could eat it, Charon let out a sound that was something between a grunt and a cough and smiled from ear to ear.

'And now you must keep your promise,' Orpheus said when he had finished.

'All right!' The smile faded rapidly from Charon's lips. 'You win. But it'll cost you one obol.'

'You said you'd take me for nothing,' Orpheus reminded him.

'Did I? I must have been mad. And you didn't make me smile all that much. A grin, perhaps. A mere simper. But if you insist . . .'

The old man moaned a great deal more, but he did take Orpheus across the river in his boat. He was still muttering to himself after he had dropped his passenger on the other side and was making the journey back.

'It was only a smirk, really. A nervous twitch. A wobble . . .'

Meanwhile, Orpheus continued along the

path, leaving the River Acheron behind him. It was strange for although he had descended many miles into the bowels of the earth, he now seemed to be outside again. He could see clouds above him where there should have been rock and the landscape, lit by a mysterious grey light, stretched far away to a distant horizon. He could just make out what looked like a castle on the very edge of the plateau and turned his steps in that direction.

Many were the strange sights he passed. Deep valleys crawling with strange hellish creatures. Further on, there was a man standing in a river beneath a fruit tree whose branches were heavy with sweet-smelling apples. The man was called Tantalus. Once he had been a king and had invited the gods to a cannibal feast. Now he suffered eternal hunger and thirst in Hades. For when he tried to reach the water to drink, it flowed away from his cupped hands. When he tried to pick the fruit, the branches lifted just out of

his reach. Now he was a skeleton, his bones glistening behind his transparent skin.

There was the giant Tityus, stretched out on the ground, his arms and legs securely fastened. He had once attempted to make love to the mother of Zeus and had been cruelly punished for his presumption. Every day two vultures landed on him, tore out his liver and ate it raw while the giant screamed in endless agony.

There was Sisyphus who had betrayed Zeus and was now forced to push a huge stone up a steep hill, only to see it slip through his hands and roll all the way back to the bottom whenever he got anywhere near the top. There was Ixion, spinning in the air on a burning wheel because he had tried to seduce Hera, the queen of the gods. And there were the Danaids, fifty women who had all killed their husbands. They had been condemned to fill a bottomless barrel with sand, a task that would take them to the end of time.

Orpheus saw many sights as cruel and as strange as these before he finally reached the castle. The doors opened as he approached and he passed through into a circular chamber paved with black marble, bare but for two silver thrones. A man and a woman sat facing him. Both were dressed in black, their skin as pale as ivory, their eyes hidden behind masks of shadow.

'Who are you?' the man demanded. His voice echoed in the empty chamber.

'My name is Orpheus.'

'Do you know who I am?'

'No.'

The man raised a hand. His fingers were long and elegant. 'I am Hades, King of the Underworld. And beside me is my lady wife, Persephone. It is rare for one who is alive to come into our presence. If that life is precious to you, tell us your purpose here in the Underworld.'

'I have come for my wife,' Orpheus said.

'Your wife?'

'The nymph, Eurydice. For many years we lived together, happily married. Then a snake bit her. Death took her from me, but I have come to claim her back.'

'That is impossible.' Hades' words rang out irrevocably. 'None has ever left our kingdom.'

'Your majesty,' Orpheus pleaded, 'I have travelled to the very extremities of the world and have crossed the last ocean to reach your land. I have suffered many hardships and sacrificed many years of my life. I have confronted Cerberus, argued with Charon and endured the sight of much pain in the land around this castle. Now, I beg you, give me what I have come for: Eurydice . . . I love her.'

'Love?' Hades' voice was cold. 'What is love? Tell me about love, Orpheus. For how can love mean anything to death?'

'Very well, your majesty,' Orpheus said. 'I will tell you about love.'

For a third time, Orpheus played his lyre, singing about love. And although the King's face remained as emotionless as a statue, Persephone was less able to hide her feelings. When Orpheus finished, her cheeks were wet with tears and she leaned over to whisper to her husband.

'Orpheus,' Hades said, and there was a strange huskiness in his voice, 'your music has moved my wife. And in truth, it has affected me. I am inclined to be merciful. Eurydice is near here, not in the plain that you have crossed – which we call Tartarus – but in the Elysian Fields, where her soul has been at rest.

'You may take her with you, back to the land of the living. Play your lyre and she will follow you, guided by the sound. But we make one condition. You are not to look on her until you both stand once again beneath the sun. You are not to turn round. Mark our words well,

Orpheus. If you turn before you reach your world, Eurydice will be gone and you will never see her again.'

Orpheus thanked the King and the Queen and left the castle, playing his lyre as he went. He played as he crossed the plain of Tartarus, looking neither behind him nor at the poor victims of Hades' wrath on either side. But even as he went, he began to wonder if Hades hadn't lied to him. Perhaps the King's show of kindness had been nothing more than a cruel trick, designed to

make him leave the Underworld alone. How could he be sure that Eurydice was behind him? He listened hard, hoping to make out the sound of her footfall, but all was silent.

He reached the River Acheron and his doubts grew. Charon was waiting to ferry him across but he neither heard Eurydice climb into the boat after him, nor felt it tip in the water with her extra weight. And what of Cerberus? The ferryman had told him that the dog allowed nobody to leave. It had to be a trick. If he took just one quick glance over his shoulder he would know. If . . .

But he forced himself to continue staring ahead. The muscles in his neck were hurting, so great was the temptation to turn his head. His fingers also ached, but he went on playing. He had no choice.

'You are not to look on her . . .'

Now he climbed the path up towards the gates of Hades. To have come so far and to lose her now would be ridiculous. And yet suppose she wasn't there? Suppose he left the Underworld and the gates closed behind him. He might not be able to get back in. He stepped out into the sun. Cerberus was still asleep. Or perhaps he was pretending to be asleep. Was Eurydice there?

'. . . until you both stand once again beneath the sun.'

He looked back.

The sun didn't shine on that side of the ocean. He glimpsed Eurydice, pale and entranced, no more than a few feet away from him. And then there was a rustle of wind. She opened her mouth. The wind took her and at once she disappeared, swept away like an autumn leaf.

The gates of the Underworld clanged shut. Orpheus fell to his knees. He had lost her for ever.

THE DEATH OF NORNAGEST

Norse

The Death of Nornagest

You may have heard that the Vikings, who terrorized Northern Europe and England during the ninth and tenth centuries, were a cruel and barbaric people, but this is not entirely the case. Although they were by nature warlike, they also had a healthy appreciation of fine art and craftsmanship. Their swords, for example, were as beautiful as they were deadly. Their ships were as elegant as they were fast. And curiously enough, as far as the Vikings were concerned, you did not have to be a great warrior to be considered a hero. You could just as easily be a poet.

This is the story of such a man – a poet and singer called Nornagest. In many ways he was the last of the Viking heroes.

His father was a nobleman, living in a small but comfortable castle. When the baby was born, he threw a banquet as was the custom. All his relatives and friends crowded round the new baby making the sort of inane comments that relatives and

friends always make on such occasions; so nobody noticed when the front door opened and three old women wrapped up in cloaks came in.

These women were the Norns, the most powerful spirits in Scandinavia. The oldest was called Urd and she was the spirit of the past. Then came Verdandi, who was the spirit of the present. The third, who wore a veil across her face, was called Skuld and she was the most feared of the Norns, for on her word hung man's future.

When the crowd saw the three Norns approaching the cot they fell silent, partly out of respect but mainly because they were afraid. Then Urd laid her wrinkled hand on the baby's head and said:

'I bless this child with good looks, and with courage that all men will one day admire.'

Then it was Verdandi's turn.

'I bless this child with the gift of poetry. Nowhere in the land will there be a greater poet.'

Finally, Skuld stepped forward.

'I . . .'

But then something terrible happened. One of the relatives, carried away by the excitement of the moment, rushed forward to pick up her little nephew who was not only going to be good-looking but a poet too. She hadn't realized that Skuld was about to speak and before anyone could stop her she had barged into the Norn and knocked her right off her feet.

Nobody spoke. The parents of the child

looked on in horror. Slowly, Skuld got to her feet. Nobody could see her face, but it was clear she was shaking with anger. For a long, long minute she stood beside the cot. Then she flung her arm out, one finger pointing at a candle that burned nearby.

'The child shall live only so long as the candle lasts,' she cried. 'When the flame of the candle flickers and dies, so will the life of the child.'

With these words, Skuld stormed out of the room with Verdandi close behind her. But Urd stayed behind. Gently, she lifted the candle out of its holder and walked over to the unhappy parents.

'A curse uttered in anger can still be made into a blessing,' she said. She blew the candle out. 'Keep the candle safe,' she continued. 'So long as the candle remains unlit, so will your child live in health and happiness.'

Then she put the candle down and followed her sisters out.

After that, the parents called the child Nornagest which means 'protected by the Norns'.

At the Court of King Olaf

Nornagest grew up and, as the two Norns had predicted, he became well-known for his good looks and much admired for his poetry. In those days, poetry wasn't something you just read in dusty books or talked about in school. It lived. With the wind rattling the shutters and the flames leaping in the hearth, Nornagest would sing of gods and heroes, accompanying himself on his harp. Even without music, his voice could somehow turn the stories into songs.

For one hundred years Nornagest travelled the country. He sang of Odin and of Thor, of the mischievous Loki and the beautiful Freya. Everywhere he went, he breathed new life into the ancient myths and legends of the Vikings. As he spoke, the furnaces of Volund the blacksmith glowed once again, the eternal city of Asgard rose out of the ashes of time and the Volsungs strode forth to renew their adventures.

But in that one hundred years, things began to change. A new religion was sweeping across Europe, a religion that declared that there was only one God. For this was the age of Christianity, and although it was taught with kindness and inspiration in some parts of the world, it was forced on the people with great cruelty in others. Idols were smashed and temples destroyed. Men and women were tortured and driven out of their homes. Slowly,

the old gods began to disappear.

One of the cruellest of the new Christians was King Olaf Tryggvason who ruled Norway from AD 997 to 1000. It was to his court that Nornagest one day came. The poet was warmly greeted and after a good dinner he set up his harp in one corner of the assembly room and began to sing. His voice was as sweet as ever because in one hundred years he had hardly aged at all.

But King Olaf did not like what he heard. He was himself an elderly man with a tuft of silver hair on each side of an otherwise bald head. He had loose, rubbery lips and the bright, watery eyes of a fanatic. He had devoted his whole life – and a great many other people's deaths – to the new religion. It was all he ever thought about. And now he heard neither music nor poetry. He heard only the names of the old gods whom he had sworn to destroy. So when Nornagest paused between two songs, the king went over to him and, sticking his chest out and fixing a superior look on his face, addressed him thus:

'My dear boy,' he said, 'I do enjoy a nice song after supper, but I notice that you sing only of Asgard and all that stuff. Very amusing, I'm sure, but of course nobody believes in it any more – not in this day and age. At least, I assume you don't believe in it.'

Nornagest narrowed his eyes but said nothing.

'Now that I come to think of it,' the king continued, 'I can't remember if you've been converted to the new religion or not. Would you care to remind me?'

'I am what I am,' Nornagest said. 'And I am happy.'

'Happy?' King Olaf cried. 'My dear fellow, you would be much, much happier if you converted, really you would. I've never been so happy. Ask anyone.'

Once again Nornagest said nothing, and now the king grew angry.

'Of course,' he said, 'you could choose not to convert. But I don't think that would be a very happy decision.' He gave Nornagest an ugly look. 'Not unless you think you can play the harp without fingers and sing without a tongue.'

Nornagest was brave, but he was no fool. He knew that, if he refused, the king would mutilate him as he had threatened. So, nodding his head sadly, he agreed that he would renounce the old gods, forget the old myths and convert to the new religion.

'Hallelujah!' King Olaf cried. 'Another soul has been saved!'

He turned and began to walk back to the throne, but then he stopped. He had remembered the story of the candle – for after that disastrous banquet the tale had been told throughout the country. Nornagest himself had heard it from his mother, who had entrusted him with the precious candle a few years before she died.

'This candle of yours,' King Olaf said, rubbing his chin thoughtfully. 'Do you have it with you?'

'I carry it always, sire,' Nornagest said.

'Well, why don't you light it before you continue to sing? It is after all rather dark in this corner. Light the candle.'

'But—' Nornagest began.

'You have converted!' the king exclaimed. 'You no longer believe in these stupid stories of spirits and magic candles. Light it and sing or my torturers will soon have you singing another tune!'

Nornagest had no choice. He lit the candle and as the king sat down on his throne, he began to sing for the last time. There were about a hundred people in the room. They had been enjoying themselves until the king's interruption, but the atmosphere had changed. They had all been converted too.

They also had denounced the old gods, disclaimed the old legends. Now their eyes flickered from the poet to the candle and back to the poet. The wax dripped. Nornagest's voice grew weaker. A breeze caught the flame and he shivered. Lower and lower burned the wick. Soon his voice was so quiet that it could hardly be heard.

But still he sang and as he sang he reflected on the changing world and the new order of

things and his voice was sad.

There was a soft hiss and the candle went out.

'There you are,' King Olaf said. 'The candle's out and the boy's still fine. What did I tell you?'

Nornagest fell to the ground.

A hundred pairs of eyes turned to the king who squirmed on his throne.

Nornagest was dead.

THE SEVEN POMEGRANATE SEEDS

Greek

Demeter was one of the more gentle goddesses who inhabited Mount Olympus. Not for her were the jealous rages of Hera, the whip-like chastity of Artemis or the burning passions of Aphrodite. Demeter was the goddess of agriculture and of marriage. Her hair was the colour of wheat at harvest-time and her eyes were a pastel blue. She delighted in bright colours, often wearing brilliant ribbons and carrying a golden torch.

Only once did she really lose her temper. This was when she discovered that the beautiful trees in a grove that was sacred to her were being cut down by a foolhardy young man called

Erysichthon. Perhaps he was some sort of early town planner, but whatever his reason for this act of vandalism, Demeter appeared to him disguised as a mortal and asked him if he would be so kind as to stop. His answer was short and unfriendly.

Then Demeter assumed her own form and punished Erysichthon in a way that was truly horrible. She condemned him to remain hungry for ever, no matter how much he ate. From that moment on, he seldom stopped. At dinner that same night, he astonished his parents by eating not only his food but theirs too – as well as that of their seventeen guests. In the weeks that followed, he ate so much that his weeping father was forced to throw him out of the house, no longer able to afford his keep. And yet the more he ate, the thinner and hungrier he got until, in the end, he became a beggar, shuffling pathetically along in rags, still stuffing himself with the filth he found in the streets.

This, then, was the full extent of Demeter's anger. But most people would agree that Erysichthon only got what he deserved. For the unnecessary destruction of a tree is a terrible crime.

Demeter had a daughter called Core (later on, her name was changed to Persephone) whom she loved more than anything in the world. Unfortunately, another of the gods also loved the girl, although in a very different way. This was Hades, the shadowy lord of the Underworld, the god of death.

Hades had spent virtually his whole life underground and his skin was pale and cold. No light shone in his eyes, eyes that had seldom seen the sun. And yet he had seen an image of Core, magically reflected in an ebony pool and he had lost his heart to her. So great was his love that he took a rare leave of absence from the Underworld, travelling to Olympus. There he came before Zeus and demanded that he give Core to him as a wife.

The demand somewhat embarrassed the king of the gods. For although he did not want to offend Hades, who was his brother, Zeus could not let him have what he wanted. For Core was his daughter. He had fallen in love with Demeter some years before and Core had been the result. If he were to send the girl to the Underworld, Demeter would never forgive him. Moreover, it would hardly be fair to condemn his own daughter to such a gloomy place – for the kingdom of Hades was such a dull and dismal land. But

on the other hand,
what was he to say to Hades,
who was older than he and . . .?

'I'll think about it,' Zeus said.

And promptly forgot all about it.

When it became clear that he was not
going to get a satisfactory answer out of
Zeus, Hades decided to take things into his
own hands.

'He did not say I could have the girl,' he reasoned to himself. 'But nor did he say that I could not. And surely, if something is not forbidden, then it must be allowed. Of course it must! In which case, Core shall become Persephone and as Persephone she will be my wife.'

And so it was that two days later, Core found herself kidnapped by the grim god of death. She was living in Sicily at the time and was out in the fields with some of her friends, collecting wild flowers for a feast that same evening. Noticing a particularly bright narcissus, she leaned down to pick it. Suddenly the ground trembled. As the blood drained from her face and her friends screamed, dropping their baskets and scattering in all directions, a great chasm appeared in front of her, yawning like a black mouth. Desperately, Core tried to keep her balance. But then a white hand that smelt of damp earth stretched out and grabbed hold of her, pulling her forward. With a hopeless

cry, she tumbled forward, disappearing into the chasm. The ground trembled again, then closed up as suddenly as it had opened. Only a jagged line, zig-zagging through the flowers, showed what had happened.

When Demeter discovered that Core was missing, her grief was overwhelming. Almost overnight she changed. No longer did she wear ribbons and bright colours. No more was her laughter heard in the fields. Covering herself with a dark veil, she flew round the world on a search that would take her nine days and nine nights. Not once did she stop for food or for drink – nor even to rest. Her only thought was for her daughter. She visited Sicily, Colonus, Hermione, Crete, Pisa, Lerna . . . nobody had seen the girl, nor was there any sign that she had been there.

At last she went in desperation to Helios, the god who every day followed the sun, riding across the heavens in a golden chariot drawn by four white horses. Nothing ever escaped the eye of Helios. Soaring in an arc, high above the world, he could see everything. And what he had to tell Demeter chilled her heart.

'You must forget Core,' he said. 'Core exists no longer. Look, if you will, for Persephone – destroyer of men – for that is what she has become as wife of the king of death. Yes! Hades has stolen her from you. Never again will you see her. Where she is now, deep in the shadows of the Underworld, she is lost even from the sight of Helios.'

At once Demeter went to Zeus. White with anger and haggard after her nine days of fasting, she was almost unrecognizable and the king of the gods squirmed in front of her.

'I didn't say Hades could take her,' he muttered.

'Did you say he couldn't?'

'Well . . .'

'I want her back, Zeus. You will return her to me!'

'I can't!' The king of the gods almost wept

with frustration. 'You know the rules. If she has eaten so much as a mouthful of the food of the dead, she is stuck in the Underworld for ever.'

'She won't have eaten. She can't have eaten.'

'And anyway,' Zeus went on, 'you know Hades. There's no arguing with him. He has to have his own way . . .'

'Very well,' Demeter cried. 'Until my daughter is returned to me, no tree on earth will yield fruit. No plants will grow. The soil will remain barren. The animals will starve. Such is the curse of an unhappy mother. Bring her back, Zeus. Or mankind will perish!'

So began a year of unrelenting famine. The crops withered and even the grass turned brown and rotted. As Demeter had promised, the animals, unable to find fodder, died by the hundred, their bloated carcasses dotting the arid landscape.

At last the situation became so desperate that Hermes, the messenger-god, was sent down to the Underworld to bring Persephone back.

'Never!' Hades exclaimed. 'I love her. I will never relinquish her.'

'But does she love you?' Hermes asked.

'She . . . she will learn to. In time.'

'But there is no time,' Hermes said. 'Her mother, Demeter, is destroying the world in her grief. If you do not release Persephone, mankind will come to an end.'

'Why should the extinction of mankind be of any concern to the god of death?' Hades asked.

'Because even death depends on life. Nothing can continue without it.'

The king of the Underworld thought long and hard but then he nodded his head.

'You speak the truth,' he said. 'Very well. It seems that I am defeated. My wife, my Persephone . . . she must go.'

And he turned his head, bringing his hand up to cover his eyes.

When Persephone heard that she was to

be returned to the world of the living, she was so happy that she laughed and cried at the same time. But one of the gardeners of Hades, a man by the name of Ascalaphus, also heard the news and at once he crept off and, changing into his best clothes, knelt before Hades.

'Oh ghastly and glorious master!' he said, rubbing his hands together in front of his chin. 'Dread lord of the Underworld, grotesque king of the dead, sovereign of the—'

'Get on with it!' Hades commanded.

'Of course! Of course!' The gardener laughed nervously. 'I just thought you'd like to know that your wife, the good and delicious lady Persephone, has tasted the food of the dead.'

'That's impossible,' Hades said. 'She has refused to eat since the day I brought her here. Not so much as a crust of bread has passed her lips.'

'I'm sure. I'm sure. But something less

than a crust of bread has, noble king. With my own eyes I saw her eat seven pomegranate seeds. In the garden. I saw her.'

Then the eyes of Hades lit up. 'If this is true,' he said, 'you shall be rewarded.

'Rewarded?' Ascalaphus licked his lips. 'Well, I didn't do it for the reward. But if there is a reward. Well . . .'

'Follow her to the surface,' Hades said. 'Do what must be done.'

So when Hermes took Persephone with him in his chariot, Ascalaphus rode on the back, unseen by either of them, dreaming of his new career (for he had never liked gardening very much) perhaps as secretary to Hades or perhaps as palace librarian or even – who could say? – as the next prince of Hell. And no sooner had Demeter received her daughter in a joyful embrace than he stepped forward with a crooked smile.

'Persephone has eaten the food of the dead,' he cried. 'She must return with me to the Underworld. There's nothing any of you lot can do about it. It's the law.'

'Is this true?' Demeter asked.

Then tears sprang to Persephone's eyes and she sank to her knees.

'Yes, mother,' she whispered. 'I ate seven pomegranate seeds. But that was all I ate. Although I was one year in that horrible place, that was the only food that passed my lips. Surely it doesn't count. Surely . . .'

But by now Demeter was weeping too.

'You have eaten the food of the dead,' she said. 'Though mankind will die when they take you from me, there is nothing I can do.'

When the gods heard what had happened, they held a great conference to discuss what should be done. On the one hand, nobody wanted the world to end. But nor could they allow Persephone to remain in the land of the living. At last, a compromise was reached and both Persephone and Demeter were called before the throne of Zeus.

'We've come to an agreement,' Zeus explained. 'And I hope it satisfies you because it really is the best we can do. Listen. What would you say if we allowed Persephone to stay in the world for six months of the year, provided she spent the other six months with Hades in the Underworld?'

Demeter thought for a moment. 'Make it nine months with me and three months with Hades and I will agree,' she said.

'Very well. You've got a deal.'

At once the famine ended. Nine months later, Persephone went back to begin her spell in the Underworld, and although she was never a truly loving wife to Hades, she was never unkind to him.

The miserable Ascalaphus never received the reward he had been hoping for. For Persephone punished him for his treachery by pushing him into a small hole and covering him with an ornamental rockery complete with flowering hibiscus border and fish-pond.

In this way he was condemned to spend the rest of eternity not only in the garden but under it too.

This myth explains why it is that for three months every year, the cold season comes and it looks as though the world has gone into mourning. Then the trees lose their leaves, nothing will grow and, like Demeter, we look forward to the spring. For it is only in the spring, when Persephone is released

from her dark confinement, that the warmth and the colours will return and we can all – god and man – celebrate the return of life.

THE WISHES OF SAVITRI

Indian

The Wishes of Savitri

Savitri was the name of an Indian princess whose devotion to her husband went far beyond the realms of normal human experience. For she was prepared to fight with death itself to regain her love and although there are those today who would call her 'old-fashioned' and 'unliberated', in her own time she was much admired as a woman and as a wife.

When she was eighteen, her father – the old king Ashwapati – suggested that she should marry, as was the custom. He was, in truth, a little concerned that as yet his daughter had received no proposals, for she was a quiet girl who preferred to read and to study her devotions than to go out dancing and enjoying herself. But Savitri gently declined.

'My dear father,' she said. 'I am not yet ready to marry. First let me travel for a year, praying at the shrines and listening to the words of the holy men so that I may draw closer to the Guardian Spirit.'

'But Savitri,' the king replied, 'you are eighteen. You are of marrying age.'

'I am young enough,' Savitri laughed. 'When I come back from my pilgrimage, if nobody has turned up you'll be welcome to arrange something for me. But perhaps these matters are best left to destiny. You'll see. If I am to be married, destiny will find me a husband.'

And so it was. Savitri wandered for a year, meeting with holy men up and down the country. She ate the simplest food and slept under the stars. To meet her, none would have guessed that she was a princess for she had left the fineries of palace life far behind her.

Eventually her travels brought her to a forest where she chanced to see a tall, handsome man carrying an axe in one hand and a bundle of firewood in the other. At first she thought he was nothing more than a huntsman or forester but there was something about him – the nobility of his bearing perhaps – that made her think again. Despite the roughness of his clothes and the meanness of his occupation, she could not help but wonder if, like herself, he was not royally born, and out of sheer curiosity (or at least, she assured herself that it was only curiosity) she asked him to tell her about himself.

'Madam,' the young man said. 'My name is Satyavan. Once I lived in a great palace, surrounded by stewards and servants. My father was the king, but in his old age, he lost his sight. Then his courtiers were able to conspire against him and – alas that I was not old enough to defend him – he was overthrown and banished. Now we live in poverty, in a small cottage in the forest. It is a hard life . . . not so much for me, but it is very hard for my poor father. I am taking him this wood now. I wish that I could bring him something that would comfort him more!'

When Savitri returned to her own palace, the joy of her arrival turned to astonishment when she announced that she intended to marry the man she had met in the forest – and dismay when the name of her fiancé was revealed. For there was in the palace a holy man called Narada who knew everything that there was to know.

'You must not marry this Satyavan,' he said.

'Why not?' Savitri asked.

'Because the unfortunate young man is living under a curse. One year from now you will be not a wife but a widow. Yes! Satyavan has only twelve months to live.'

Now every Hindu woman desires to die before her husband and when the princess heard this news her face went pale. But she had already plighted herself to Satyavan and did not intend to break her word. Try though her father and Narada might to dissuade her, she insisted on going ahead with the marriage.

And so the wedding was proclaimed. An iron ring was bound on Savitri's left wrist and her veil was tied to the cloak of Satyavan, as custom dictated. A sacred fire was lit and hand in hand they walked around it seven times while a priest chanted the ancient prayers. Then she put away all her jewels and fine clothes and went to live in the

forest as the devoted wife of Satyavan and the dutiful daughter of his parents.

Never once did she tell her husband what Narada had foreseen, but never for a minute could she forget it. If Satyavan had an appointment with the god of death, then nothing could come between the two of them. For it is often said in India that Yama, the god of death, is the only god who never breaks his word and that if something is absolutely certain, then it is 'as true as death'. For this reason, Yama is also known as the god of truth and of faith.

And after twelve months, he came.

Savitri and Satyavan were walking in the forest together. It was a beautiful summer's day, the grass a soft green beneath their feet and the sun showering them with emeralds as it broke through the leafy roof. She was carrying a basket filled with wild fruit. He, as ever, carried his axe – for even in the warm weather he liked to keep the stores of firewood well supplied. He had been

working while Savitri sang to him, when suddenly he stopped and complained that he was dizzy. A moment later he dropped the axe and staggered. Suddenly cold with dread, Savitri ran to him, and she caught him just as he fell, fainting into her lap.

There was a rustle in the undergrowth and it seemed as if a cloud had passed across the face of the sun for the glade was thrown into shadow. When Savitri looked up she saw a figure dressed in black, a noose of rough rope clasped in one hand. He looked at her with a sad expression and nodded. Then she knew that this was Yama and that he had come for her husband.

'Savitri,' he said, and his voice was strangely musical, like a song in a minor key. 'I claim the soul of Satyavan as is my right. Do not be afraid for him. All his sorrows are now over.'

He leaned down and fastened the rope around the dying man's head, his hand brushing against the flowing locks of hair that only that morning had lain on the pillow beside her. At the touch of the rope, the soul of Satyavan separated from his body, standing up to follow Yama.

'Farewell,' Yama said. 'And remember – I am the only god to whom everyone is faithful. One day you and I will meet again.'

He turned and walked away but, driven by an instinct that made her forget her fear, Savitri followed. She followed him through the forest and into a second clearing where a waterfall splashed down into a rocky pool. Hearing her, Yama turned again and now two black flames flickered where his eyes should have been, for his head had become a skull and his body, beneath the robes, a bare skeleton. But Savitri was not afraid.

'Still here!' Yama exclaimed. 'I see that you have more courage than sense, for who would willingly follow the god of death? Very well – I will give you a gift to help soothe your grief. You may ask for anything you like except for the life of your husband.'

'Then I ask for my father-in-law's sight to be returned,' Savitri said.

'It is granted,' Yama said. 'Now farewell again.'

For a second time, the god of death walked away, leading the soul of Satyavan behind him on the rope. Now the forest grew wild. Thistles sprung up and thorns pressed in on the path. Wild bats flitted in the air and owls hooted mysteriously in the shadows. But still Savitri followed, and when Yama looked back, there she still was.

'I shall give you another wish,' Yama said, and now his voice was angry. 'It is as much to dissuade you from this folly as to reward you for your devotion to your dead husband. But once again you may not ask for his life. Anything but that!'

'Then I would like my father-in-law's kingdom and his wealth to be returned to him,' Savitri said.

'It is done. Now leave me!'

But Savitri, believing herself to be almost

a friend of death's, followed on. The forest grew ever darker and more savage. Now strange figures could be glimpsed gliding silently between the trees. A foul-smelling swamp bubbled nearby, tentacles of white mist spreading out over the ground.

'Still here!' exclaimed Yama in all his fury when he turned round for a third time. 'Never has a mortal so defied me! And a woman! A woman with the courage of ten men it would seem. Very well! One last wish will I grant you but then you and I must part company, lest I decide to keep you in my shadowy kingdom for all eternity. What will you have this time? So far you have favoured only your father-in-law. Now what can I give you for yourself?'

'Only this,' Savitri said. 'Grant that I may have many children and that I should live to see their children's children grow up in health and happiness. Will you give me this, great Yama?'

'It is a good wish,' Yama said with a smile.

'And I grant it.'

Then it was Savitri's turn to smile. 'You have forgotten,' she said, 'that according to Hindu law, a widow does not remarry.'

Yama thought for a moment, realizing how he had been tricked. If Savitri could not remarry, then how could she have children and grandchildren? And yet that was what he had promised her, he who never broke his word. In which case . . .

For a second, Savitri thought the god of death was going to strike her down where she stood, but then the forest rang with the sound of his laughter and he pulled the noose from around Satyavan's neck.

'It is a courageous woman who would follow her husband into the grave,' he said. 'And it is a cunning woman who would trick the god of death himself. Very well, Savitri. I will give you back the only man who can be the father of your children. And it will be a long, long time before the two of us meet again. Go in peace, for your devotion to Satyavan has defeated me.'

Savitri and Satyavan returned to their cottage to discover that the sight and the fortunes of the old king had indeed been restored. And thus began a long and happy life in which the two were always true to one another. As true, indeed, as death.

NIDUD THE CRUEL

Norse

Nidud the Cruel

One of the cruellest kings who ruled in the northern lands many hundreds of years ago went by the unusual name of Nidud. As a small boy he had probably been the sort who pulled the legs off flies. As an old man he certainly took pleasure in pulling them off people. If you were a servant in the palace of King Nidud and you spilt a glass of wine, you might well end up being flogged to death – and you would consider yourself lucky that the king was in such a good mood. For King Nidud's cruelty knew no bounds. Everybody, even his wife, called him Nidud the Cruel. And many a long evening in the palace was spent talking (or whispering, rather) of his latest act of cruelty.

Now it happened that one day King Nidud heard talk of an ironworker who was said to be descended from the elves and who lived in a house some distance from the palace. This craftsman, whose name was Volund, was known throughout the world for the beauty and delicacy of his workmanship with gold, silver and bronze.

Like many cruel men, Nidud loved jewellery and ornaments – not to admire them but simply to possess them. And when he heard about Volund, he decided at once that the craftsman should become his slave and spend the rest of his life working only for him. So he sent his soldiers out to search for Volund, to capture him and to bring him back to the palace. And this is what they did.

They came upon Volund as he lay asleep, dreaming of Hervor who had once been his wife but who had one day turned into a swan and flown away from home. Seven hundred gold rings lay on the workbench beside his bed, each one more finely wrought than any jewellery in the world. When the soldiers saw the rings, they seized them and threw them into a sack. Then they did exactly the same to Volund. And the next thing the craftsman knew, he was standing in front of the cruel

king and
his cruel wife
and sons.

'Well, blacksmith,'
Nidud said, fingering one of
the gold rings, 'this isn't a bad
piece of work. Not bad at all.'

'It is mine,' Volund said quietly. 'Give
it back to me.'

'It was yours,' the king corrected him with
an ugly smile. 'Now it is mine. And so are
you, blacksmith. From now on, until the day
you die, you will work as my slave, making
nice things for me.'

'Never!' Volund cried.

At this, the king's face grew dark with anger. There was nothing Nidud hated more than someone who refused to be afraid of him. And if that someone was young and handsome, as Volund undoubtedly was, it only made it worse. For the king was old, with bloodshot eyes, a flabby face and a drooping moustache. He was also secretly a coward. So Volund was everything he was not. And that was why he hated him.

'Take him away!' the king commanded. 'And set him on the tiny island of Saevarstad where he will be surrounded by water and unable to escape.'

'May I make a suggestion?' the queen asked.

'Of course, my little bundle of poison.'

'Have the sinews of his knee-joints severed. That way he won't be able to walk, let alone swim.'

The king and his two sons laughed heartily at this suggestion. They laughed as Volund was dragged away. And they laughed all the

louder when they heard his cries of pain.

So it was that Volund found himself on a rocky island surrounded by grey sky and rough sea. They had built a house with a forge and a hard wooden bed for him, but there was nothing else there for his comfort. Although he could walk a little, it was only with great pain and anyway, there was nowhere for him to go. The island was so small that he could see from one side to the other. Nothing grew there. It was always cold and wet.

Every day, a servant would row out from the palace bringing with him gold, silver and bronze, the raw materials of Volund's work. If the ironworker had made the king something beautiful the day before, the servant would also bring food. If not, he would starve. That way, Volund was forced to work and in his palace King Nidud became the envy of all his friends as more and more priceless ornaments appeared around him.

But Volund had elfin blood in his veins. He did not despair. Instead, he dreamed of escape and in a short time he had formed a plan. He could not walk but, with all his skills, perhaps he could learn to fly. And so he began to build himself a pair of wings, with feathers made of brass beaten paper thin and struts of solid silver. Every night, after he had finished working for the king, he would turn to the wings and slowly, slowly, they began to take shape.

The one person in the palace who took no pleasure in the growing pile of jewellery was Bodvild, the king's only daughter. She was less cruel than the rest of the family (and for that reason, something of a disappointment to her father) and had fallen in love with Volund the moment she had seen him. One day, finding an excuse, she went out in the rowing boat and came to his house while he was working on a pair of golden candlesticks.

'What can I do for you, princess?' Volund asked when he saw her.

'My ring is too loose,' she said, stretching out one finger.

The blacksmith flinched when he saw it, for she was wearing one of the rings that he had crafted for his wife.

'I want you to tighten it,' Bodvild continued.

'Give it to me and I will see to it for you.'

Volund took the ring and set to work while the princess sat and gazed at him. If the two of them had been able to read each other's minds, they would have been most surprised.

'How handsome he is,' Bodvild thought. 'His hair is so fair and his eyes so blue. Until my father had his knee-joints cut and locked him up here he would have been strong and fast, but even after all his suffering, he still bears himself like a prince. How could my father do such a thing to him? He is so young, so gentle . . .'

'I could kill her,' Volund thought. 'I could revenge myself on her father by taking my hammer and striking her dead. And why not? Although she is only a girl, the blood in her veins is the same blood as that of her wretched family. Yes. I will kill her and then I will throw her body into the sea . . .'

Clutching the hammer, Volund turned round.

'I love you, Volund,' the princess said. 'And I hate my father for what he has done to you.'

When he heard these words, Volund

smiled to himself. It was not a very pleasant smile. For he realized that Princess Bodvild had lost her heart to him and that there was no need to kill her for she would always be his.

'Leave me,' he said, quietly.

'I cannot,' Bodvild wept. 'I hate my parents for their cruelty. I have no family now. I have only you and without you I am lost.'

'Then you are lost,' the ironworker said. 'For knowing who your parents are, I cannot look on you except with hatred.'

Bodvild fled from the house to begin the slowest death of all – the death of unrequited love. The colour drained out of her skin and her hair turned grey. She ate so little that her bones stood out. Her voice faded away to a whisper. Soon she was no more than a ghost, wandering around her father's palace with eyes that were always red with weeping.

King Nidud noticed the change in his daughter but didn't know either what had caused it or what to do about it. He did think of whipping her to try to cheer her up, or at the very least to cheer himself up, but he never got round to doing it, because by this time he had other things on his mind. His two sons had disappeared – and although Nidud had never shown much kindness to anyone or anything in his life, he was genuinely fond of his sons.

'What can have happened to them?' he asked the queen one evening over supper. 'It's not like them just to . . . disappear.'

'They're probably hunting or fishing,' the queen said.

'I'll have them whipped when they get back,' Nidud growled. 'And I'll have Bodvild whipped at the same time. Look at her! Sitting there moaning all the time. Anyone would think—'

'Don't upset yourself, my dear,' the queen interrupted. 'Here – have some wine. These are the new drinking cups that Volund has sent us. Aren't they beautiful?'

'Yes,' the king muttered, taking the cup in his hand. As the queen had said, it was very beautiful, although unusually large for a cup. In fact, it was just about the size of a human skull.

'Where can they have got to?' Nidud sighed, sipping his wine.

'They can look after themselves,' the queen said, lifting her cup. 'They've got their heads screwed on the right way.'

They drank in silence, the

queen running her fingers over the new necklace that Volund had sent along with the two cups. It was a very unusual necklace having just four circular stones on it, each one about the size of a human eyeball.

'Do you like it?' she asked.

'Like what?' Nidud said.

'My new necklace. For some reason it reminds me of my two boys. I can't wait to show it to them. I'm sure their eyes will pop out of their heads.'

Princess Bodvild, sitting at the far end of the table, had said nothing throughout the meal. Now the queen turned on her angrily.

'There's no need to be so sulky,' she snapped. 'After all, you got a new present this morning too. A lovely brooch.'

It was true that the princess was wearing a lovely new brooch although that too was a little unusual. It was made with about fifty nuggets of gold, each one about the size of a human tooth.

'You really ought to be more grateful,' the queen continued. 'You should never look a gift-horse in the mouth.'

But despite the wonderful gifts that Volund had made for them, the three of them weren't at all happy. When the night watchman came in to report that there was still no sign of the boys, he had the unfortunate man taken out and hanged. Shortly before midnight they all went to bed. An hour later, the storm broke.

Nidud the Cruel

It came sweeping in over the sea. First the wind raced round the palace, then the clouds were torn apart by a writhing serpent of lightning and finally the rain lashed down. King Nidud was woken up by a clap of thunder so loud that, as he sat up in his bed, his ears rang. It was a terrible night. Looking out of his window he could see nothing but the swirl of water flashing silver against the immense blackness of the night. Trembling, he sat alone in the chamber, his knees hunched up under his chin, his hands clutching the sheets.

There was a movement just outside the window and King Nidud whimpered. In those days there was no glass in the windows and he was certain that there was some horrible monster out there in the storm about to fly in and devour him. There was another flash of lightning and he glimpsed a great pair of wings, bright gold in colour, beating against the raging wind. He wanted to hide under the sheets, but he was so afraid he could not

T·YEATES

move. Then, with another crash of thunder, the creature flew right through the window and stood at the foot of his bed.

'Help!' King Nidud screamed. 'Help! It's a monster! There's a monster in my room!'

The door flew open and the queen, wrapped in a dressing gown, hurried in.

Volund the Ironworker, wearing the fabulous bronze wings which he had built for himself, the water running out of his hair, pointed a finger at the king.

'It is true that there is a monster here,' he said. 'It is a monster of cruelty, a monster of inhumanity. And its name is King Nidud.'

The queen opened her mouth to speak, but Volund continued quickly.

'Tonight I leave you,' he said. 'No man will ever see me again. But before I go, I must tell you how I have repaid your cruelty.

'Your daughter's heart is broken. That was not my doing. But she hates you now, as much as she loves me and you have lost her for ever. You have also lost your sons . . .'

'Where are they?' Nidud croaked.

'They are here, in the palace,' Volund laughed. 'Or at least, they are here in part. They came over to my island, King Nidud. They wanted me to make them swords of gold and so they came secretly, even as your daughter had done. I killed your two sons, Nidud, to revenge myself on you. I buried their bodies beneath the forge, but first I made drinking-cups out of their skulls, a necklace out of their eyes and a brooch out of their teeth. See what your cruelty has led to! Tonight you have drunk wine out of the skulls of your children.'

Then the queen laughed hysterically as her sanity left her for ever. She screamed with laughter while the king wept and cursed. And Volund stepped back out of the window to be swallowed up by the storm, leaving the wretched couple to a life of misery and madness.

FIVE VISIONS OF HELL

Do you ever wonder where you'll go when you die? (I do sometimes think about this and as long as the answer's not Luton Airport, I don't mind.) What happens to people after death is one of the great questions facing humanity, and because, of course, there's no answer, it has created some extraordinary stories. In fact every culture from around the world has imagined its own 'underworld' to which the souls of the dead travel once life has ended.

HEL'S BELLE & VALHALLA

In Norse myth those brave warriors who fell gloriously in battle were sent to Valhalla, a majestic banqueting hall decked out in gold, where they could drink and feast and tell tales of their courage and strength to the end of time. Everyone else went to Hel.

Hel was a dark, damp, dismal place covered

in mist. It was found in the distant land of Niflheim, at the lowest level of the universe, and was ruled over by a monstrous hag, also called Hel, who dwelt in a great mansion with high walls and giant gates, attended by her monstrous servants and the souls of the dead.

THE LORDS OF DEATH

The Mayans of Central America believed in a vast underground city they called Xibalba, or the 'Place of Fright', which was reigned over by several extremely unpleasant death lords. New arrivals were sentenced to a series of deadly trials and tortures, forcing them to walk through houses filled with razors, bats or hungry jaguars.

But first you had to get there, and that wasn't much fun either.

First off you had to cross a river filled with scorpions, followed by a river of blood and a river of pus. Next you would arrive at a crossroads, where each of the four roads would speak aloud, deliberately confusing you as to which path to take. The hope was that you would get lost forever. And if you did arrive, you would be invited to take a seat. Unfortunately this was actually a hotplate, which would cause hideous injuries and make you feel you had died a second time. Death, for the Mayans, was definitely not nice.

SOULS OF THE DAMNED

The ancient Greeks believed in the land of Hades, deep within the bowels of the earth, a subterranean world divided into various regions through which the souls of the dead had to travel. It was ruled over by the god Hades, who shared his name with his dark kingdom.

The first stop on the way to the land of the dead was the Acheron, the river of woe, where travellers would have to pay the wizened old boatman to ferry them across. (This is why the Ancient Greeks always put coins in the eyes of the recently departed. It was so they could pay the ferryman.)

Once on the far shore the souls of the dead would find themselves face to face with

Cerberus, a monstrous hound with three fearsome heads and a snake for a tail, who guarded the gates of Hades so that nobody could escape.

The regions of Hades included the Elysian Fields, a place of wild flowers and gentle breezes. Not surprisingly this area was reserved for the souls of the virtuous and heroic, who would spend eternity in joyful comfort. Next came the Asphodel Meadows, which was a bit like the world above. Those who had been neither very good nor very bad would live here, engaging in boring daily chores. Finally there was Tartarus, a terrible place wrapped in three layers of night, where sinners and evil men were sent by the god Hades to endure punishments too cruel and unpleasant to describe.

THE CIRCLES OF HELL

In the fourteenth century the Italian poet Dante wrote *The Divine Comedy*, in which he described a terrifying vision of the underworld. The gateway to this Hell famously read: 'Abandon

Hope All Ye Who Enter Here'!

In Dante's version Hell is divided into nine Circles, each lower than the last, and the souls of dead sinners are sent to whichever level corresponds with the crime they have committed.

The various levels are populated by vicious demons with whips, and winged monsters with human heads. The Minotaur is there, and Cerberus too, each guarding the entrance to another Circle. At the very centre of the ninth and final Circle, which is reserved for those who have betrayed their friends or families, stands the Devil himself, a three-headed giant who weeps bitter tears and chews forever on the heads of traitors.

THE BONE EATER

The ancient Egyptians believed that the souls of the dead would be judged by the god Anubis, who had the body of a man and the head of a jackal. He would rip out their heart and weigh it on a set of scales.

If you had been wicked during your life, you would be fed to a charming creature called Ammit. Part lioness and part hippopotamus, with the head of a crocodile, Ammit was also known as 'Devourer of the Dead' or 'Bone Eater'.

However, if your heart weighed just the right amount, you were allowed to continue on to Aaru, a heavenly paradise of fertile reed fields, where the sun ended its journey through the underworld and resurfaced in the eastern sky. Very different to Luton Airport.